Robin Klein
Illustrated by Alison Lester

for Michael and Sue

OXFORD UNIVERSITY PRESS
Melbourne   Oxford   Auckland

mily Forbes and her mother lived in the top flat, and Mrs McIlvray, the owner, lived in the bottom one. Pets weren't allowed in the flats—it was a very strict rule. Mrs McIlvray always stared at Emily severely when they met on the stairs. She looked as though she suspected Emily of smuggling guinea pigs upstairs in her school-dress pocket.

Emily's mother was very understanding. She didn't say irritating things like, 'Never mind, just pretend your nightie-bag pup is a real one.' Or, 'When you grow up you can have a farm with lots of animals.' She said, 'I just don't know how you can bear it, Emily! It's terrible! I just don't know how you can stand not having a pet!' Which made Emily feel noble and courageous.

It wasn't easy to look pleasant or interested when kids at school talked about their Labrador dog and how he could fetch the morning paper, or their grey Persian cat which let itself be worn as a neck scarf.

A gift shop near her school had pet rocks, with little plastic eyes glued on them, advertised for sale in the window. Having a rock for a pet seemed better than nothing at all. Emily didn't have fifty cents to buy one of the shop-window rocks, so she started inspecting the ground everywhere she went.

Rocks weren't plentiful in that suburb, and the huge ones in the park opposite the flats had been placed there by a crane. Emily knew she wouldn't be able to get one of those up the stairs by herself.

Then one day she found a beautiful rock. It wasn't anywhere special—the bulldozer working on the new sports oval near her school had scooped it up with a load of soil. Emily picked it up and rubbed it clean with the sleeve of her school jumper.

The rock was a cosy, rounded shape, and a gleaming, rich dark brown, the colour of Vegemite in a new jar before anyone shoves a knife in to spread their toast. Emily took it home and put it on the living-room table, propping it up with a lemon squeezer because it was so smooth it tended to roll away.

'Mrs McIlvray couldn't possibly complain about your keeping a rock for a pet,' said Emily's mother. 'What are you going to call it?'

'I'll call it Thing,' said Emily. 'It's nice and short and easy to remember.' She patted the rock goodnight and went to bed.

rs Forbes, who was inclined to be vague about such matters, forgot to turn off the oil heater, and when they got up in the morning the living-room was like a sauna.

'Oh blah!' said Emily. 'The heat cracked Thing.'

'Rocks don't crack as easily as that,' said her mother. 'Let me look.' She picked it up and found that there *was* a crack, like an opening zip-fastener, and while she was looking it zipped open even more. The rock quivered in her hands, and made a peculiar slithery noise. Mrs Forbes made a louder one, and dropped it nervously on to the carpet.

Emily was more curious than alarmed, and she poked at the rock with the point of an HB pencil. Something inside tapped back, so she helpfully tugged the two sections of the rock shell apart. A creature wriggled out, uncoiled itself and blinked at them. It was about half a metre long and a most attractive shade of green, like a Granny Smith apple.

'What on earth can it be?' asked Emily's mother. 'I never saw anything like it before!'

'We did a project on dinosaurs at school,' said Emily. 'I think this could be a baby stegosaurus. They weren't as awful as those dinosaurs they have in horror movies, though. I think they were vegetarians.'

'Oh,' said Mrs Forbes, relieved. 'You can give it that left-over coleslaw in the fridge, then.'

'Come along, Thing,' said Emily, and the little stegosaurus followed her into the kitchen. He ate the coleslaw, and four ripe bananas Mrs Forbes was saving to use for banana custard, and half a carton of mango yoghurt. While he was eating, he thumped his tail enthusiastically on the floor.

'If you keep him, you must tie newspapers round his tail to muffle the noise,' said Mrs Forbes. 'It's going to be difficult hiding him from Mrs McIlvray. I think they grow to quite a large size, Emily. Still, I suppose you can deal with each problem as it comes up.'

The first problem for Emily was the worry about Thing being left on his own while she was at school and her mother was at work. Luckily she discovered that he liked television. While she was having her breakfast, she had the set switched on. Thing looked at it with great interest, then he jumped up on the couch and kneaded his little claws in and out of the couch cushions, making a contented purring noise. So Emily left the set turned on, with the sound very low.

When she came home from school, Thing was still on the couch, watching TV. He seemed to have grown a little during the day. Emily fed him a bunch of silverbeet which she had bought at the greengrocer's on the way home.

Mrs Forbes phoned from where she worked, as she did every day to make sure Emily got home safely.

'That stegosaurus should really be getting some outdoor exercise,' she said. 'I don't think dinosaurs just sat around watching TV in prehistoric times. You'll have to smuggle him out into the park, but don't let Mrs McIlvray see you both. And make sure no one notices you in the park, either, Emily. People can be very mean about animals being a nuisance. They're quite likely to whisk Thing off to a museum and put him in a glass box with a label.'

Thing seemed to understand the need for quiet, even though he was so young. He padded softly after Emily down the stairs, and curled up his tail so that it wouldn't bump from one step to the next.

There weren't any people in the park, and Thing loved it there. He munched weeds and chased after autumn leaves, and rolled over for Emily to tickle his tummy. Then he sat down in the park fountain and gargled.

The only dangerous time was when a young man in a track suit went by, jogging. He blinked and slowed down. 'Freeze, Thing!' whispered Emily, and Thing froze to look just the same as the rocks in the fountain, only mossier, so the young man jogged on.

When it was time to go back to the flat, Thing followed Emily obediently, and she got him upstairs without being seen. But soon there was a knock on the door, and Mrs McIlvray stood outside, looking indignant.

'You've gone and brought a Saint Bernard dog in off the street!' she said. 'The rule here, young lady, is NO PETS!'

'We don't have a Saint Bernard dog,' Emily said truthfully.

'There are large muddy footprints on the steps, and they lead right up to this door!'

'Oh, they must be from my new plastic flippers,' Emily said, not so truthfully. 'I was testing them out in the park fountain. I'm sorry, and I'll wipe up the marks straight away.'

'Kindly don't let it happen again,' said Mrs McIlvray.

Emily didn't. She always took two pairs of old woollen socks and put them on Thing before she sneaked him back up the stairs after his daily ten minutes in the park.

Thing was really very little trouble. He spent all day watching television, with the tip of his tail in his mouth at the exciting bits. He didn't seem to mind what programs were on. He liked them all: cartoons, classical music concerts, the news and weather forecasts, and even talks on gardening and cookery demonstrations.

At night he slept in a soft bed Emily made from a rubber inner tyre tube she got from the corner garage, and an old duffel coat she didn't wear anymore. Thing didn't care that it wasn't a nice, soggy, prehistoric marsh. He circled once or twice then settled down cosily with his nose resting on the tip of his tail.

He had a double row of boney plates down his back, and Emily kept them beautifully polished with Brasso. He grew to about the size of a small rhinoceros, and then stopped growing. Emily's mother was very relieved.

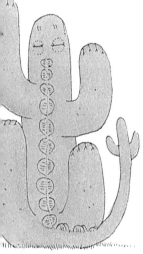

Thing liked living at Emily's place and being taken for walks. He became very clever at freezing into various shapes when necessary. He could make himself look like an ornamental fence, or a very large cactus on a nature strip. Emily was careful to take him for outings at times when there would be very few people about. The closest he came to being discovered was when they were out skateboarding early one Sunday morning.

They skated up and down the deserted shopping centre. Thing was too large and too heavy to ride the skateboard, of course, but he liked batting it along with his nose while Emily balanced on it.

A group of people from an adult landscape painting class arrived to sketch the buildings. Thing hurriedly froze into a free-form sculpture in front of the council library, and Emily sat protectively on his tail and pretended to be adjusting the wheels on the skateboard.

'What an interesting sculpture!' said the artists, poking at him, and standing back with their heads on one side, looking most intelligent. 'How very modern and unusual. And what marvellous texture the sculptor has managed to achieve with fibreglass!' Emily wished they would go away.

'It's not a free-form sculpture at all,' said an elderly woman in a floral painting smock. 'It's a young stegosaurus.'

But nobody believed her, and Thing tried to stay frozen for a long time while the artists wandered all over the empty shopping centre practising how to sketch perspective. He was as stiff and creaky as a glacier when Emily was able to take him back to the flat.

ever mind,' said Emily. 'We'll have a nice little game of kick-the-carton-the-groceries-came-in. Your goal is the couch, and mine's the kitchen door.'

Thing was very good at that game, and he never cheated, either, although he had a tail he could have used, and Emily didn't. The game was very exciting, with five goals each, and they forgot to be quiet. Emily's mother was out, because she sometimes earned extra money at weekends driving taxis, so she wasn't there to remind them about Mrs McIlvray. Soon there was an angry knock on the door.

'Freeze Thing!' whispered Emily, and he froze into the shape of a coffee-table. Emily reluctantly opened the door.

'I'm sorry about the noise, Mrs McIlvray,' she said. 'I was practising ballet.'

Mrs McIlvray looked past her into the living-room, which had become rather disarranged during the game of kick-the-carton. 'I thought ballet was supposed to be pretty and graceful and quiet,' she said frostily. 'And that is a very odd coffee-table you have there. Made out of green concrete, too. I don't think I can allow you to have concrete furniture in this flat. It might damage the floors.' She came inside and peered critically at Thing, who had his head tucked under his stomach, and his tail tucked under to meet it. 'It's not even very well designed, either,' said Mrs McIlvray. 'I should know, as I collect antique furniture, and I am an expert about good design. What are all those odd flaps sticking up on the surface? Most illogical, if you ask me!' She put on her reading glasses to examine Thing more closely, and tweaked the blades along his spine. She was very surprised when they moved.

'They're specially made like that.' Emily said quickly. 'They're to hold magazines and dried flower arrangements and cups of coffee.'

'I really don't know how your mother could have bought such a frightful table,' said Mrs McIlvray. 'Just look at those heavy thick legs! They'll wear down the pile on my carpet. You must tell your mother that this thing has got to go back to wherever it came from!'

Thing heard, and was dreadfully upset. He remembered being in the rock egg at the sports oval, which hadn't been nearly as nice as Emily's place. He unfroze, whimpering, and scuttled over to Emily and hid his face in the front of her windcheater.

'It's a sort of mechanical table,' Emily said desperately. 'It can be used as a dish-trolley.'

'You naughty little girl!' scolded Mrs McIlvray. 'You know very well it's a nasty extinct animal of some kind! I'm certainly not having a dinosaur living in my block of flats! It belongs in a glass case in a museum. I'll give you until tomorrow night to arrange for its removal. And what's more, it has to stay out in the back yard while you're at school and your mother is at work. But it has to be gone by tomorrow evening!'

Emily felt so sad she could hardly bear it. Her mother, when she came home, went downstairs to plead with Mrs McIlvray, but it was useless. They gave Thing a wonderful feast of every vegetable and fruit they had in the kitchen, and let him stay up past midnight to watch the late night movie. But in the morning, Mrs McIlvray made them put him out in the back yard.

mily went to school, crying so hard she had to pretend she had hay fever, and Thing stayed in the back yard. There was nothing happening there except leaves falling from Mrs McIlvray's maple tree, and he wondered why Emily hadn't brought down his TV set and plugged it in. He didn't like being in the yard very much. He chased after the drifting leaves, and played with the handle of the rotary clothes hoist.

Mrs McIlvray came out and scolded him sharply. She wound down the handle so tightly that it couldn't budge, and then she went out shopping. Thing looked wistfully over the front fence, but he knew he wasn't allowed to go out there without Emily to tell him when to freeze.

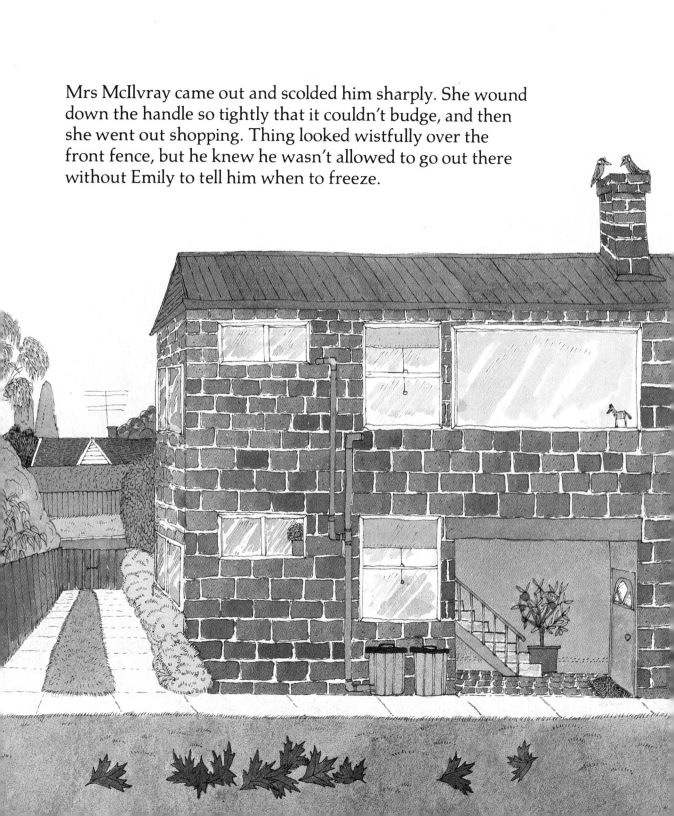

While Mrs McIlvray was away, a van was driven into the driveway of the flats, and two men got out. Thing quickly froze into something that looked like a length of pebbled patio. The men didn't knock at the door, or open it with a key. Instead, they pulled up the rubbish bin and stood on it and pushed in a flywire screen window to climb into the ground floor flat. Then they opened the door from the inside. After a while they came out carrying Mrs McIlvray's fur coat and her stereo record player and her new electric freezer. They put them into the van and went back inside the flats again.

They came out with Mrs McIlvray's antique oak writing-desk, which was extremely valuable, and her jewel box, and Emily's mother's electric sewing-machine. Thing was delighted to see the sewing-machine being taken away.

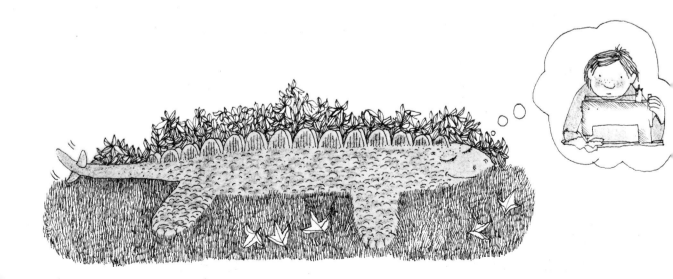

Emily had to make an apron to pass a school craft examination, and she wasn't very good at sewing. She always looked glum while she was pinning on bias binding, and sewing it, and then unpicking it again because she had sewn it on back to front. Thing didn't like to see her look miserable.

The two men went inside and came out with Mrs McIlvray's antique jade and ivory statues and her 19th century clock, and put them in the van. On their last trip of all they came out with Thing's TV set.

Thing wagged his tail, because he thought these men might kindly plug it in somewhere, and he could watch all the afternoon programs instead of chasing maple leaves. But they put the TV set in the van with all the other items they had removed from Mrs McIlvray's flat and from Emily and her mother's flat. Then they shut the door of the van.

Thing unfroze a great deal more. He knew that his TV set contained cowboy movies, and Yoga five-minute exercises, and How to Grow Better Roses, and Fred Flintstone, and everything he liked to watch, and he wasn't going to let anyone take all that away.

He unfroze completely, went around behind the van, and tried to open the door with his nose. When that didn't work, he stretched out his neck and nudged the two men very politely.

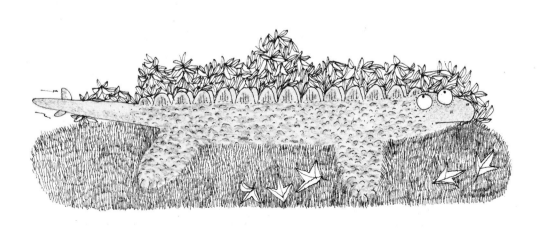

One of them turned ivory and the other one turned jade, just like Mrs McIlvray's antique ornaments, and they leapt into the van and slammed the doors shut. They rolled up the windows at a tremendous speed, sealing themselves in like canned sardines.

They couldn't back their van out into the street, because Thing took up a great deal of space. He sat down and waited patiently for them to get out and unpack his TV set, so they just sat in the van and looked very upset and unhappy.

hing was still sitting and waiting when Mrs McIlvray returned from shopping. At first she looked annoyed to see that he had got into her driveway, but then she noticed the broken flywire screen and the van crammed with all her valuable possessions. She dropped her basket and ran down the street to fetch the constable from the police station.

'We've been trying to catch those two burglars for months,' the constable said. 'They're a wicked, scheming, crafty, slippery pair of crooks. I'll take them down to the police station, and then I'll come back for the van. But would you kindly ask your dinosaur to step aside out of the way?'

The two burglars didn't look wicked or scheming when they had to step over Thing's tail and be taken down to the police station — they looked pale and worried.

Mrs McIlvray opened the van door and began to take her antiques inside, and Thing sat very quietly and humbly, with his tail tucked out of the way so he wouldn't be a nuisance. But when Mrs McIlvray finished, she didn't look at him crossly — she bent down and patted him on the head.

'You needn't sit out in the draughty yard,' she said, 'you can wait in my flat until Emily gets home from school.'

Thing wagged his tail and followed her inside, carrying his TV set in his mouth. Mrs McIlvray plugged it in and switched it on for him. He watched all his favourite afternoon shows, and when there was a demonstration on how to fold Origami paper into interesting shapes, Mrs McIlvray even cut up some bright gift-wrapping paper so he could practise. She kept telling him how grateful she was that he had saved all her precious belongings.

When Emily came home, still looking very hayfeverish, Thing was helping Mrs McIlvray unpack her shopping and stack it away in the right shelves. 'I'm sorry he got out of the back yard,' Emily said dolefully. 'And I couldn't find any kid who'd give him a good home. Everyone's mothers said no they couldn't. No one seems to want a stegosaurus. I guess I'll just have to telephone the museum.'

She couldn't bear to look at Thing. It was heartbreaking to think of your best friend permanently frozen in a labelled glass box. She looked instead at Mrs McIlvray, who was making a very expensive salad of broccoli and eggplant and avocado pear, decorated with little radish roses. Mrs McIlvray put the bowl of elegant salad on the floor in front of Thing.

STEGOSAURUS (extinct)

'Museum?' she said indignantly. 'What on earth are you talking about, Emily? If you don't mind my mentioning it, dear, this dinosaur of yours watches far too much television. It can't be very good for him. While you're at school during the day, I'll take him for a nice healthy run in the park—after we've had our lunch.'

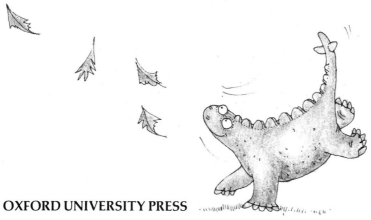

OXFORD UNIVERSITY PRESS

Oxford London Glasgow New York Toronto
Delhi Bombay Calcutta Madras Karachi
Kuala Lumpur Singapore Hong Kong Tokyo
Nairobi Dar es Salaam Cape Town
Melbourne Auckland
and associates in
Beirut Berlin Ibadan Mexico City Nicosia

OXFORD is a trademark of Oxford University Press.

First published 1982
Reprinted 1983 three times
Reprinted in this edition 1984

NATIONAL LIBRARY OF AUSTRALIA CATALOGUING IN
PUBLICATION DATA

Klein, Robin.
   Thing.

   For children.
   First published: Melbourne: Oxford University Press
   ISBN 0 19 554549 4

   I. Lester, Alison. II. Title.

A823'.3

TYPESET BY DAVEY LITHO GRAPHICS PTY LTD
PRINTED IN HONG KONG BY HIP SHING OFFSET PRINTING FACTORY
PUBLISHED BY OXFORD UNIVERSITY PRESS, 7 BOWEN CRESCENT, MELBOURNE